For George
M.W.

For Samuel
V.A.

First U.S. miniature edition 1993
First published in Great Britain in 1992
by Walker Books Ltd., London.

ISBN 1-56402-256-0 (miniature)

Library of Congress Catalog Card Number 91-71822
Library of Congress Cataloging-in-Publication information is available.

10 9 8 7 6 5 4 3 2 1

Printed and bound in Singapore

Candlewick Press
2067 Massachusetts Avenue
Cambridge, Massachusetts 02140

Sailor Bear

by
Martin Waddell

illustrated by
Virginia Austin

CANDLEWICK PRESS
CAMBRIDGE, MASSACHUSETTS

Small Bear was a bear
in a sailor suit
who was lost
and had no one to play with.
"Now what shall I do?"
wondered Small Bear.

He thought and he thought.
Then he looked at his suit,
and he *knew* what to do.

"I'll be a sailor and sail on the sea!"
decided Small Bear.
But he didn't have a boat.
"Now what shall I do?"
wondered Small Bear.

He thought and he thought.
Then he looked at the sea,
and he *knew* what to do.

"I'll go and get one!"
decided Small Bear.
He went to the harbor,
but the boats there
were too big for a bear.
"Now what shall I do?"
wondered Small Bear.

He thought and he thought.
Then he looked around the shore,
and he *knew* what to do.

"Small bears need small boats,
so I'll make one!"
decided Small Bear.
He made a boat
from some pieces of wood
and half a barrel.
He called it "Bear's Boat,"
and he took it down to the sea.
BUT . . .

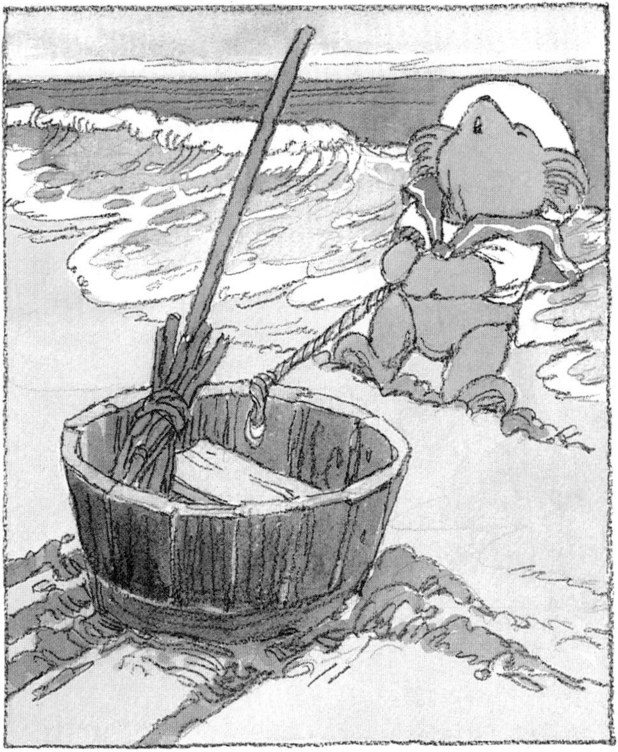

the sea looked too big for his boat.
"Now what shall I do?" wondered Small Bear.

He thought and he thought. Then he looked
at a puddle, and he *knew* what to do.

"Small boats need small seas,
so I'll find one!"
decided Small Bear.
He went to the park,
where he found a small sea,
AND . . .

Small Bear sailed in "Bear's Boat"

by the light of the moon. BUT . . .

the sea grew too rough! "Bear's Boat" rocked

and it rolled and it shattered and SANK!

So he swam and swam until he reached the shore

where he lay on a rock all shivering and cold.

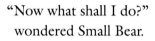

"Now what shall I do?"
wondered Small Bear.

He thought and he thought.
Then he sighed at the moon,
for he didn't know what to do!
"I'm sick of the sea,
so I think I'll give up!"
decided Small Bear with a sniff.
He curled up by the rock
and went sadly to sleep all alone.

The very next morning a little girl
came and found Small Bear,
and she hugged him
and took him home
and set him to dry by the fire.
"Now what shall I do?"
wondered Small Bear.

He thought and he thought.
Then he looked around the home,
and he *knew* what to do.

"I'm FOUND,
   and I have someone to play with,
   so I'll stay where I am!"
   decided Small Bear,
   and he cuddled up
   close to the girl
   and he stayed . . .

. . . and he never went back to the sea!